Hi, I'm Ruby.
Have you ever felt frustrated? Frustrated is the way you feel when
something doesn't go the way you want it to.

When I feel frustrated, I feel really tight in my body. Sometimes my head feels
hot, and it's hard to make it stop. Do you ever feel that way? Everybody feels
frustrated sometimes. This book is about a girl named Sally who learned how
to move through her frustrated feelings, just like you can learn to do.

Ready? Let's read! I can't wait to see you again at the end of this book...

A Note to Parents and Teachers

Helping children develop a basic understanding of their feelings is one of our most important jobs as parents and educators. When children are able to access, understand, and express what they feel, they sail more smoothly through their days, playing, socializing and cooperating.

Frustration is an intense experience for young children. Parenting experts advise allowing children to feel their frustration and learn to move through it, rather than making it go away or trying to avoid it altogether. This skill builds resilience and character that help children navigate their lives for years to come.

Research shows that supporting emotional literacy in children before age five sets them up for more success in school, in relationships, and in life. It is our goal at The Mother Company to present children with beautiful, engaging products that offer them the words and skills to become more self-aware, communicative, and cooperative. Our motto is "Helping Parents Raise Good People." We hope you find this book to be one step closer to reaching that goal.

— Abbie Schiller & Sam Kurtzman-Counter, The Mother Company Mamas

For parenting resources and "Ruby's Studio" DVDs, downloads, books, music, dolls, mobile apps & related products based in social and emotional learning for young kids, visit us at www.TheMotherCo.com.

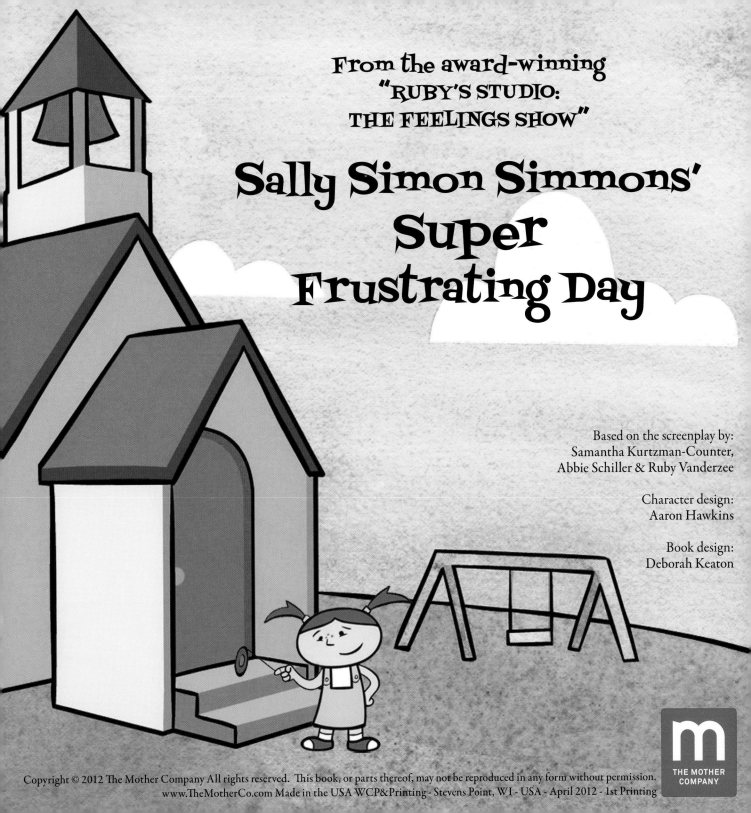

From the award-winning
"RUBY'S STUDIO:
THE FEELINGS SHOW"

Sally Simon Simmons'
Super
Frustrating Day

Based on the screenplay by:
Samantha Kurtzman-Counter,
Abbie Schiller & Ruby Vanderzee

Character design:
Aaron Hawkins

Book design:
Deborah Keaton

THE MOTHER
COMPANY

Sally Simon Simmons was a **super** special kid who brought an **extra** bunch of charm to **everything** she did.

One day at Sally's school there was a project just her style...

"It's double-decker sandwich day...Let's make one stretch a mile!"

"A double-decker sandwich?
Yessirreee, let's get down to it!
Mine is going to touch the sky!"
She knew that
she could do it!

Sally built that
SANDWICH fast,
layer after layer:
lettuce, pickles,
mustard, cheese,
each went on
with care -
lettuce, pickles,
mustard, cheese,
rose high INTO
THE AIR!

Sally kept on piling, and her sandwich got too tall- "Wibble-Wobble-Tilt!" it went -and soon began to fall!

What an awful mess I've made - who knew that mustard flies?!

Sally sat and thought:
"This time I have to make it stick-
I'll pile it even faster now.
That ought to do the trick!"

so Sally started fresh;
she was determined not to stop.

Sally Simon Simmons'
face was red
and fiery hot.
She ducked to hide
behind the mess,
happy she was not.

Sally Simon Simmons set
her frustration aside -
she sat right down, took a deep breath
and then again she **tried.**

She worked her way so slowly,
from the bottom to the top.

She took her time, made sure it stuck-
they thought she'd never stop!

Just as **Sally** made the move to set the final bread, the tower began to wobble. Would it fall and crash instead?

But Sally knew just what to do:
"I'll breathe and take it slow!
And if it falls, I did my best-
and that's the way to go!"

"It's the **tallest,** super duperest sandwich in the **world!**"

"And NOW I'm not frustrated— I'm a proud and happy girl!!"

Boys and girls, remember
Sally Simon Simmons' success:
work through your own
frustration and
just try to do your best.

I'm so glad you could join me today to explore frustration. What a big feeling! Sometimes things don't work out the way we want them to – but if we slow down, take a breath, and keep trying, we can move through our frustrated feelings.

Ready for our special good-bye?

Finger. Hand. Blow a kiss!

Remember... You are the only you in the world, and you are loved.